THE DAWN SEAL

Holly Webb
Illustrated by David Dean

LiTTLE TiGER

LONDON

"Oh, Dad! It's beautiful!" Lissa stood on the riverbank, looking at the line of boats and the sun glittering on the water.

Dad grinned at her. "Good, isn't it? Even if it is a pain having to carry everything along the path." He hefted Lissa's huge backpack further up on to his shoulder. "How much stuff did you bring, Liss…"

"I'm here the whole summer!" Lissa pointed out. "I need clothes. And Mum said she wasn't sure how easy it is to do washing on a boat."

"I do have a washing machine," Dad said.

"Everything you'd find in a normal house, actually. Just smaller. But there's not much space inside for hanging anything out to dry."

"Which boat is yours?" Lissa asked eagerly. Dad had sent her photos of his new home, but she was finding it hard to work out which one it was. There were so many boats moored along the riverbank, of all shapes and sizes. One of them looked like a battleship, only smaller. And there was even one with a tall mast and furled sails. Lissa had never thought she'd see huge sailing ships on the river.

It seemed so strange that her dad was actually living here now. The river was about as different from Lissa's street back home as she could imagine.

At first, she'd thought it was going to be weird spending her summer holidays with Dad on a barge, but now she was realizing just how exciting it could be. Still … she wished Mum was here to see the beautiful boats too. And Zoe. Zoe would love them – except she'd be bouncing around all over the place and Mum and her partner Mickey would be panicking about her falling in the river. *It probably wouldn't be a good idea to have a two-year-old on a boat,* Lissa thought.

Dad smiled. "Over there. She's called *Rose Dawn*, can you see her? The name's painted on the front."

"She?" Lissa frowned.

"All boats are called she," Dad explained. "It's traditional, I think. Even if they're called something like, I don't know, *Trevor*. Still a she."

"That's weird… Oh yes! I can see her. The blue one? Dad, she's huge!"

"What, did you think you were going to spend the summer living on a tiny rowing boat?" Dad was laughing but he sounded proud.

He loves the boat already, Lissa thought, and something tugged inside her. *Rose Dawn* was Dad's home – but perhaps that meant Lissa could belong here on the river too?

Lissa's parents had split up a few years before, but Dad had always been close by and Lissa had been able to see him almost every day, even though she was living with her mum. Now Dad had moved to this houseboat on the river, an hour's drive away. He'd explained it was something he'd wanted to do for a long time – and it would be good for him to be closer to London for work. He'd promised that they'd still see each other as much as before – more even, because Lissa would come and stay and it would be special.

But Lissa wasn't convinced, even though Dad kept saying how exciting it would be to stay with him on a boat. How could she spend as much time with her dad when she couldn't just run round the corner and knock on the door of his flat? Already she hadn't seen him for over a month, while he'd been moving in and sorting out everything on the boat… When he'd arrived to pick her up, he'd looked almost strange. It was just for a moment, while Lissa got used to his hair being longer, but it had been a bit of a shock.

Still. They were going to make up for lost time now.

"*Rose Dawn*'s a Dutch barge." Dad interrupted Lissa's thoughts, still sounding so pleased and proud. "A long time ago they were built of wood, and they were sailing boats that carried cargo around the canals in Holland. But most of the newer ones like *Rose Dawn* are metal, and they have engines instead of sails. Although she's nearly a hundred years old, so not that new!"

Dad set off down the path along the side of the river and Lissa hurried after him. A couple of the boats they passed had people sitting out on the little decks at each end, and one man was sunbathing in a chair on the path – they all waved at her and Dad, and Lissa smiled shyly back.

"Are they your neighbours?" she whispered to Dad. "Does everyone stay here all the time, or do the boats move?"

"A bit of both," Dad explained. "*Rose Dawn* has an engine, so I can move her, but I've paid for the spot where she's moored. It's a bit like renting a house, I suppose. But I could take my own house on holiday with me! I'd just set off up the river without having to do any packing. Isn't that brilliant?"

"I suppose…" Lissa agreed a bit doubtfully. She couldn't quite imagine it. Her house belonged in her street – with her friend Grace next door but one, and school just round the corner, and all the dogs and cats she liked to wave to in their different windows. It wasn't just the *house* that was home, it was the place too.

Dad juggled the bags about a bit so he could put his arm round Lissa's shoulders. "Everything's going to be OK, don't worry."

"I'm not worried *really*…"

"It must feel strange though, the thought of being away from your mum the whole summer. But we'll have fun, I promise."

Lissa nodded. She loved spending time with Dad, that wasn't the problem. But he was right, six weeks away from home was a big change.

"Here you go." Dad lifted Lissa's backpack over the side of the boat and then held out a hand to help her climb on board. Lissa stood under a sort of canopy roof and felt the boat shift beneath her feet slightly. There was water underneath her, which made her tummy feel a little odd – but Lissa didn't mind it.

"This bit's called the wheelhouse," Dad said, clambering on behind her and pointing to a polished wooden steering wheel, surrounded by complicated-looking dials and gauges. "And we go down these steps and along here into the saloon." He led Lissa down into a cosy living room, with a sofa built into the side of the boat, and a couple of armchairs. "Then this end is the kitchen – except on a boat you call it the galley."

"It's bigger than the living room in your old flat, I think," Lissa said, looking around.

Dad snorted with laughter. "I know. I really love it, Lissa. I think you will too. Want to see your cabin? We have to go back the other way – I wanted to show you the main saloon first." He beckoned her out into the narrow passageway and waved at the wooden doors. "Bathroom's over here – and that's just for you, there's another one off my cabin at the other end of the barge." Then he opened the door opposite, glancing hopefully at Lissa. "Here you go. This is one of the reasons I liked *Rose Dawn* so much. There's a whole room that you can have for your own."

Lissa peered in, not sure what to expect. She'd liked her room in Dad's flat. They'd painted it together, and Dad had let her help choose the furniture. She didn't think any of it would fit in a little boat cabin.

"Oh!" She swung round to look up at Dad. Her star-print duvet was on a high bunk bed and the space underneath had been made into a sofa. It was piled with cushions and the huge teddy bear that Dad had won for her at the funfair last summer. "It's like my high sleeper."

"I think the people who invented high sleeper beds must have got the idea from boats," Dad said. "Boat designers can fit anything anywhere. Have you seen there's a bookshelf along each end of the sofa? And there are drawers underneath it too."

"Can I sit on it?" Lissa asked, suddenly feeling shy.

"Of course you can. It's your bedroom. No one else is going to sleep in here, I promise. If any friends stay, they can sleep on the sofa in the saloon – that's the spare bedroom as well."

Lissa nodded and sat down on the edge of the sofa, picking up the big, saggy bear. He smelled of her old room. She looked slowly round the rest of the cabin. Dad was right – it was all so tidy and clever. There was a little table built into the corner with a chair tucked underneath. Dad had put the pens and pencils she'd left at the flat on there, and a Japanese waving cat he'd given her for Christmas. Lissa stretched out and tapped the cat's paw to make it wave – the cabin was so small that she could reach across, but she didn't mind. Dad had brought all her things. He'd fussed about where to put them for her. He wanted her to be happy.

"I thought the table would be good for doing

homework, if you come and stay at weekends in term time," Dad explained. "I know it's not very big… Do you like it?"

Lissa scrambled up and hugged him. "I love it!"

Lissa wasn't usually very good at unpacking when she went to stay with Dad – she was never there for very long so it was easier just to live out of a bag. But on *Rose Dawn* she couldn't do that. There wasn't enough space in her cabin to keep tripping over her huge backpack. She squashed her clothes away in the two big drawers and lined up the books she'd brought on the shelves along the sofa. She put a photo of Mum and Zoe on the shelf too.

Then she stopped to look out of the tiny round window right next to her sofa bunk. She could see out of it if she kneeled up – there was a perfect view of glittering water, and then the boats and trees on the

opposite bank. Her
view. Her own
little slice of
river. A duck
floated past,
cutting a
narrow wake
through the
water. The odd
bubble popped here
and there. Something
brownish-grey surfaced for a moment, and
then disappeared – *perhaps it was a fish*, Lissa
thought, almost pressing her nose against
the glass. She smiled to herself, feeling all
the niggly worries about staying with Dad
and missing Mum and Zoe slide away with
the deep water.

"How are you doing?" Dad looked round the cabin door. "Oh, well done, you managed to get all your stuff in. I wasn't sure if everything would fit! Do you want to come and sit up in the wheelhouse with me? I've got some biscuits."

Lissa nodded and hurried up the steps, chasing eagerly after her dad. The wheelhouse was the open bit where they'd first climbed aboard. She'd noticed it had picnic chairs and a little table. It was like a sort of outdoor living room, half open to the water. She could keep watching the river, and they could talk about the things they were going to do over the summer.

Dad had promised they could go on all sorts of fun trips. *Rose Dawn* wasn't moored on the Thames in the centre of London, but it was easy enough to get there – there was a train station close by the mooring. They could still go to museums, see a show at the theatre, and even visit the Tower of London and see the Crown Jewels. Lissa had looked up things to do in London online – Mum didn't live that far away but day trips there were a rare treat. She had made a list of all the things she wanted to see.

Dad had good biscuits, chocolate-coated and with chocolate chips. He'd made himself a cup of tea and there was a glass of blackcurrant squash for Lissa on the table. She curled herself up in the folding chair and looked about. The wheelhouse had a canopy over the top and short fabric walls, a bit like a beach windbreak. It all reminded Lissa of camping. It would be cold sitting there in the winter but on a hot day like today it was lovely. She could hear the water, gently splashing and sucking at the side of the boat, and there was a river smell. Half nice, and half not. What Mum would call *interesting*.

The splashing was because another boat was going past – a narrowboat, like *Rose Dawn* but not quite so wide. The woman steering it waved as she saw Lissa watching and Lissa waved back at her. That woman thought Lissa belonged on a boat.

Maybe she did.

"I love sitting out here," Dad said. "You get to see everyone walking along the river path, and then the boats as well. And the ducks," he added, pointing to a string of ducks who'd appeared silently along the side, looking hopeful. "I feed them toast crusts. I think they've got us marked down as a good boat to beg from now."

Lissa eyed her half-finished chocolate biscuit. She wanted to feed the ducks but she didn't really want to give it away – besides, maybe chocolate wasn't good for ducks? She knew it was bad for dogs.

Dad handed her a plate that he'd left on the counter above the wheel. "It's OK. You keep the biscuit. I saved this from breakfast."

"Thanks, Dad." Lissa crammed the biscuit into her mouth and took the plate of leftover toast. The ducks seemed to know what was going on as soon as they saw the plate and they started circling eagerly. "There's more coming," Lissa told Dad as she tore the toast into little bits. "Oh, Dad, look! Ducklings!"

Dad stood next to her. "Cute, aren't they? So small. They bob around like those plastic bath ducks. I can't imagine keeping track of them all, though… How many are there? Eight? Nine?"

"Nine, I think. They're really fluffy." Lissa threw the toast pieces, trying to aim them at the tiny brown and yellow ducklings. They were cheeping, and they sounded so hungry. But the bigger ducks were quicker and they kept snatching the crusts first.

"Hang on, I've got the end of a loaf going a bit stale." Dad disappeared down the steps into the main part of the boat and came back seconds later with a couple more slices. "OK, we need to send the big ones off over there."

He threw a few small pieces of bread further out into the river and the larger ducks raced after them, the water swirling around their fast-paddling feet. The ducklings fluttered and cheeped, and Lissa was sure they looked sad. "It's OK," she called, tearing up the second slice and throwing it down. "Here you go. But you've got to eat it fast, they'll be back any second…"

The ducklings shot here and there, gobbling up the crumbs and still squeaking excitedly. Then they gazed up at Lissa and Dad, looking for more.

"That was the last of the loaf, sorry!" Dad

held his hands up, as if he was showing the ducks they were empty. "There is actually another loaf for lunch," he whispered in Lissa's ear. "I'm just not telling them that…"

Lissa snorted with laughter as the ducklings paddled away after their mother in a long string. She saw other birds too – geese sailing

down the middle of the river, a swan standing on one leg over on the opposite bank, its head tucked under its wing. Seagulls perched on the rail of the next boat along, watching Lissa with sharp yellow eyes.

So much to see. It was going to be the best summer. Dad had promised.

Dad took Lissa for a walk along the river the next morning to admire the boats moored close by. Lissa couldn't help staring at the one that looked like a tiny bright red battleship.

"Isn't she amazing?" Dad said admiringly. "I got talking to her owner – I found out she's a lightship, or used to be. See the little tower in the middle? She was a floating lighthouse. So if there were dangerous waters where it was too deep to build a lighthouse, you could have a floating one instead."

THE DAWN SEAL

"I like the way they're all different," Lissa said as they walked on. "Much more different than houses are."

Dad nodded. "I know what you mean. I like looking at all the names. And the gardens. I need to get some plant pots for *Rose Dawn*. Maybe even a big planter that I could grow tomatoes in, or herbs. Something we can eat." He pointed out a squarish-looking boat with a whole garden planted on its roof. "Look at this one!"

"But that doesn't really look like a boat." Lissa said, frowning. "It's more like a little house on the water."

"Mmmm, that's true. I think the boats along this row are here all the time," Dad said, still admiring the flowers. "They don't have engines, so someone would have to tow them if they wanted to moor somewhere else."

"Oh, look, there's a dog on that narrowboat."

Lissa smiled at a bulldog, who was glaring at her from his own stripy chair on the back of the boat.

"He's called Jack," Dad told her. "I met him the other day. He looks grumpy because he's on a diet, his owner told me. The vet said he's a bit overweight and it's not good for his legs."

"You could have a dog, Dad," Lissa suggested hopefully. She'd been working on Mum and Mickey for ages to let them have a pet but they weren't keen. Perhaps she could convince Dad instead… "You work from home – umm, boat – almost all the time anyway. You could have a dog to keep you company."

"Tricky without a garden, I reckon," Dad said, shaking his head. "So. Tomorrow, I hope you don't mind, but we've got to go and do a supermarket shop. It won't take too long. Then the day after I've booked us in for a paddleboarding session. I thought it would be a fun thing to do together. Does that sound OK?"

Lissa nodded. "We did it with school at the end of last term. I fell in three times!"

"Oh…" Dad looked worried. "Maybe it wasn't such a good idea."

"No, it was brilliant. I loved it! I definitely want to do it again." Lissa beamed at him. "I bet you fall in more than I do."

Dad looked at the river, deep and brownish-green, and waggled his eyebrows at her. "Just you wait…"

That night, Lissa settled into her top bunk, hugging her pillow. Dad had warned her to be careful not to sit up too fast in case she banged her head on the ceiling, but she didn't think she would. She wasn't very good at waking up in the morning – it always took

her ages. She *never* sat up quickly in bed. The
bunk was cosy, and she could hear the river
out of the little window, which was open at
the top. The water sloshed gently against the
side of the boat and there was just the faintest
rocking motion, almost too slight to notice.
But she loved it.

The river felt welcoming, Lissa decided.
Almost as if it were looking after her. And
that was even after Dad had kept on telling
her how careful she needed to be on board,
and that she mustn't take any silly risks with
the water.

She had been worrying about this strange
new life that Dad had started on a boat, so
far away from home and everything she was
used to. But now she was actually here, it
was starting to feel like an adventure they

were going on together.

Lissa yawned and started to make a shopping list in her head for tomorrow. She'd checked out Dad's kitchen – the galley, he said it was called – and there was hardly any food in it. Partly that was because the galley had only two cupboards, so you couldn't store much, but mostly it was because Dad was very boring when it came to eating. He actually *liked* plain cornflakes. They needed more biscuits, because they'd finished the packet when they got back from their morning walk. Definitely more exciting cereal. Bananas. Cheese for sandwiches...

Lissa settled into sleep, curled as tightly as the ducks roosting along the river path. She shouldn't have worried. *Rose Dawn* was already feeling like her home too.

Then, on the third day of the holidays, Dad ruined everything.

Lissa had trailed sleepily into the saloon, expecting to see Dad eating his breakfast, only to find it empty. She had been looking forward to trying her new chocolate cereal – a holiday treat – and to teasing her dad some more about how many times he was going to fall in. The paddleboarding session was at ten, and Dad had said the water sports centre was not far down the river, so there was no rush, but Lissa still wondered where he was.

She grabbed a bowl and opened the cereal, pouring herself a big helping and admiring the way the milk went all chocolatey. She guessed Dad must be in the wheelhouse, eating his breakfast, looking at the river.

But when she went to look, the wheelhouse was empty too. Rosy, who owned Jack the grumpy bulldog, was walking along the river path, with Jack stomping slowly along behind her. Rosy rolled her eyes at Lissa.

"Dogs are supposed to like walks… No one told Jack that."

Lissa grinned. It was nice that Rosy knew who she was. But where was Dad?

She went back into the saloon and then tiptoed through to the main cabin at the stern end, where Dad slept. Perhaps he was having a lie-in? He'd told Lissa before that he didn't much like mornings. It was one of the good things about working freelance, he'd said. He didn't have to get up early to go to work, since he mostly worked from home and decided his own hours.

THE DAWN SEAL

The door was half open and Lissa peered round it, expecting to see Dad as a long lump under the duvet. But instead he was already working, sitting on the bed, propped up against the pillows, with a laptop resting on his legs.

"You're awake!" He smiled at Lissa, but he looked tired and a bit worried.

"I've been looking all over for you."

"Yes… Sorry. I should have sorted out breakfast first." Dad glanced down at the screen again, as though he couldn't tear himself away from it, and Lissa felt worry bloom inside her. Dad was caught up in a work project, she could tell. He'd explained that he was going to have to do some work while she was staying, but he would be able to get most of it done after Lissa was in bed. It wouldn't get in the way of him spending time with her, he'd promised.

That was one of the reasons Dad had said it would be so good for Lissa to live on the boat with him that summer. If she'd stayed at home with Mum, she'd have had to go to holiday club at least some of the time, since Mum and Mickey needed to work, and Zoe was going to her childminder.

Lissa felt her hands tighten on the cereal bowl. They were going paddleboarding. They were going on trips. Dad wasn't going to be working all day. He'd *said*.

Dad set the laptop down on the bed and sat up properly. He was smiling, but he looked as though only half of his mind was on talking to Lissa. The rest of it was thinking about the project he was working on.

"I'm really sorry, Lissa. I got asked to take on a last-minute job. It's for someone I've worked with before. They pay really well and I don't want to let them down. Don't worry, though, it's not going to be a problem. Just a bit more work than I thought I'd need to do, that's all. It won't change anything."

Lissa nodded. "OK…" She could hear how small her voice was, how doubtful it sounded. But she wasn't sure if Dad could hear that. "I was just having some breakfast." She showed him the bowl. "The new cereal's really nice. Do you want some?"

"Oh… No, I'd better just get this done, love, sorry."

"I'll get dressed, then. But I wasn't sure what to put on for paddleboarding. Do I have to wear anything special? What time do we need to leave?"

Dad blinked and Lissa felt the worry inside her grow into something more. He'd forgotten. "Paddleboarding? Oh yes, of course." He rubbed his eyes. Lissa could see him thinking, trying to work out what to do. "Right."

Lissa didn't say anything. She wanted to shout – she could feel the words pushing up from inside her. *You knew it was today!*

We talked about it only yesterday, you said how excited you were! You promised it would be really fun. You were teasing me about falling in… But she held them all in and stood silently watching. Perhaps if she didn't say anything, Dad would sort it out somehow. He'd make the work wait and say it didn't matter. If she made a fuss, she definitely wouldn't get what she wanted. Dad would give her that disappointed look and say that his work was important, and she had to understand… Getting upset and angry made it easier for him to brush her away.

"You need to wear your swimming costume," Dad murmured, frowning slightly. "They'll give you a wetsuit and boots at the centre, and a buoyancy aid, and everything else you need. But … um … Lissa, I don't think I'll be able to come with you after all. I really need to get this bit of work done today." Dad ran his hands back through his hair and gave her an apologetic look.

"Oh," Lissa whispered. She'd known deep down he was going to say that – but a tiny bit of her had still hoped…

"I'll drop you off there, of course."

She nodded.

"And I'm sure we can book another session for both of us. In a couple of weeks, when I've finished this work."

A couple of weeks? Lissa swallowed hard.

She had been so looking forward to spending time with Dad – and now it wasn't going to happen.

"I'm really sorry, Lissie… I wish I could have said no, but buying *Rose Dawn*, and moving… All of it cost a lot. I can't turn down work just now."

Lissa turned away. "I'll find my swimming costume," she muttered.

She should have known it was too good to be true.

Lissa looked around the group of people standing on the edge of the water. Everyone seemed a bit nervous, apart from three girls who were obviously friends as they'd come together and weren't listening to anything the instructor was saying.

Most of the group were older than she was, but there was a boy who seemed to be about her age. He looked grumpy – a bit like Lissa felt. Dad had dropped her off, still apologizing

and promising to make it up to her, and Lissa
was trying to believe him, but it was hard.

She could have thrown a strop and said she
wasn't going to do the session without him,
but what would be the point? She'd seen loads
of people kayaking and paddleboarding down
the river, and she'd been looking forward
to doing it herself. She'd enjoyed her time
paddleboarding with school, but it would be
even better here, when they'd have a board
each instead of one huge one with about six
people jumping in and messing around and an
instructor doing most of the work. She wanted
to splash about and feel the river slopping over
her toes.

Lissa had been living on the river for nearly
three days. She'd leaned over the side of *Rose
Dawn* and trailed her fingers in the water.

She'd teetered a couple of times climbing on to the barge, eyeing that strange, dark channel between it and the bank. But she didn't feel as if she'd been properly close to the water yet. She wanted to be *in* the river, not *on* it.

She was really looking forward to getting closer to the water creatures too. All those interesting bubbles and splashes she kept seeing – they had to be big fish, surely? And there were the ducks, and the heron she'd spotted…

The water sports centre was in a sort of backwater – Lissa thought that was the right word. It was a quiet side channel, overgrown with trees. It split off from the main river, separated by a little island, just a narrow strip of trees, like a tiny forest in the middle of the river. There were huge red signs saying the water wasn't deep enough for boats, so it was

perfect for people learning paddleboarding
and kayaking – nothing big was going to come
lumbering through.

The instructor – her name was Milli –
explained that it was easiest to start off with
kneeling on the board, just to get used to
the feel of it. She led them down the slipway
and showed them the leashes that fastened
round their ankles with Velcro. *That's good*,
Lissa thought. She couldn't lose the board
completely, at least. She just needed to
remember to keep hold of the paddle. She
gripped it tightly, trying not to be nervous.
The water looked darker in the side channel,
shadowy with the reflections of the trees, and
the whole place was quiet and mysterious.
There were sunny patches here and there too,
Lissa pointed out to herself.

She scrambled on to her board in one go, refusing to let the nerves get to her.

"That's it, Lissa, great!" Milli called. "Now try out your paddle. Right hand on the top if you're paddling on the right of your board. Go for it!"

Lissa kneeled up, feeling the board rock and wobble beneath her. But she felt surprisingly safe, even surrounded by dark water.

She dipped the paddle in and pulled it back, grinning to herself as she felt the board move forwards. She was doing it! It was working!

Lissa paddled a couple more strokes and realized she was turning round in a circle. She needed to swap sides. She was just moving the paddle over to the other side of the board when there was a panicked yelp behind her, and a huge splash. Lissa tried to look to see what was happening and felt her board tip dangerously. She yelped too – and did a spectacular slow-motion slide and splash into the river.

The grumpy-looking boy was behind her, waist-deep in water and trying to catch his paddle. He looked embarrassed now instead of grumpy, and his fairish hair was plastered dark and flat down his face.

"Sorry," he muttered at Lissa, trying to push his hair out of his eyes. "I didn't mean to make you fall in."

He really did seem sorry, so Lissa shrugged. "I probably would have gone in as soon as I tried to stand up. I did paddleboarding with school a few weeks ago and we all kept falling in. Standing up is hard."

The boy nodded, looking relieved. Maybe he'd thought she was about to have a go at him. "Yeah, that's what I was trying to do. Kneeling felt OK but the board just slid out from underneath me when I got up."

He looked at his board uncertainly, obviously wondering how he was going to get back on. Milli was over by the riverbank, still encouraging the three chatty girls, who seemed unsure about getting on their boards at all. She waved at them and called, "Never mind, Lissa and Alfie! Are you two OK scrambling back on yourselves? You were doing really well! Don't forget to stay between the marked posts, yeah?"

Lissa waved back, smiling at Milli to show she was fine. She wasn't totally sure how she was getting back on but there was no way she was going to ask for help.

"If I hold your board still, maybe you could climb on?" the boy – Alfie – suggested. "Then I could push my board next to you and you hold it for me?"

Lissa nodded. "All right." If the board

was steady and not wobbling around, she reckoned she could do it. Alfie grabbed one side of her board and Lissa pulled herself up on the other. She felt a bit like a wet fish, heaving herself on, but she made it. "That was quite easy, actually," she told him, kneeling up. "Here, push your board over so I can grab it." She caught hold of the edge and gripped it as tightly as she could. "It's a bit hard to hold on to. Try now."

Lissa was pleased to see that Alfie looked just as silly trying to get back on his board as she thought she had, but he managed it at last. "Thanks," he panted.

They both sat on their boards for a bit. "I'm going to stick to kneeling right now," Lissa said.

"Yeah, me too. Want to try going under

those trees?" Alfie suggested, dipping his
paddle in.

Those trees are willows, Lissa thought. Their
long, yellow-green branches trailed in the
water and the way they leaned over from

both sides of the channel gave the whole place the feel of a mysterious, leafy tunnel.

"That island looks cool," she said to Alfie. "I wonder if anyone ever lived on it."

Alfie eyed the wooded island doubtfully. "Only ducks, I reckon. I suppose you could camp on it. But no one ever has. It's not really big enough to be exciting and there's no water or anything." He rolled his eyes as he saw Lissa staring pointedly at the river. "You know what I mean! No water you could drink. You'd have to boil river water. They told us in Cubs, you can't just drink it."

"No loos either," Lissa agreed. "It would be fun for a bit, though. Like having your own private island to explore."

"It wouldn't take much exploring. It's tiny. But yeah, it would be fun." Alfie made a face. "And it would definitely be peaceful. We've got a new baby at home and he screams all the time."

Lissa nodded. "I remember that from when my mum had my sister. It's tough."

"It's worse because we live on a houseboat," Alfie explained. "There's no escape. And the boat's not that big so there's baby stuff everywhere." He looked along the river and pointed. "Look, our boat's just round that bend in the river. She's called *Anastasia* because it's my mum's favourite name."

It turned out that Alfie lived on one of the squarish-looking boats not far down the river from *Rose Dawn* – the ones that Lissa had thought were too much like houses to be very interesting. But she didn't say that to him.

"We're almost neighbours," Alfie pointed out. He looked quite happy about it. "I've seen your dad's boat, I think. She looks nice."

"She is," Lissa agreed. "It's a bit weird though. He hasn't had her for very long and before that he lived in a normal flat. I don't know a lot about boats." She sighed and then burst out, "He said we were going to learn about living on the river together, but now he's got this big work project to do. He was supposed to be coming paddleboarding with me today. He forgot all about it." She snapped her mouth shut, feeling embarrassed. She hadn't meant to say all that to Alfie – she didn't even know him! But she had to say it to *someone*.

Alfie sniffed. "I'm doing this so I'll be out of the way. Mum and Dad are too busy looking after Joshua – that's his name, my baby brother. He's quite cute, when he's not screaming."

Lissa stole a sideways glance at Alfie. He was digging his paddle into the water extra hard – she was having to paddle fast to keep up with him.

"Maybe they just need to get used to having a baby?" she said hesitantly.

"Maybe." Alfie shrugged as if he didn't care, but Lissa thought he might be more upset about his mum and dad and Joshua than he was letting on.

"Let's try standing up again," she suggested, more to distract Alfie from feeling miserable than because she really wanted to. She pushed herself up with one hand and wobbled on to her feet, beaming triumphantly at Alfie. "I did it, look!"

"OK, OK." Alfie stood up too, probably a bit too quickly, given how much he swayed sideways, but he stayed standing. "Hey, cool! We did it!"

"Now we've got to paddle," Lissa pointed out. Somehow the handle felt shorter than it had before and she wasn't quite sure where to put her hands. Still – the worst that could happen was that she fell in the water again.

"Hey, look…" Alfie pointed across the water to a Canada goose, its black neck glossy in the sunlight. Swimming beside it were three tiny grey goslings, their feathers so fine and fluffy that they looked like fur.

"They're so sweet," Lissa said. The goslings didn't seem to have noticed her and Alfie. That was the best bit about paddleboarding, Lissa decided. It was so quiet – you could just skim over the water, dipping the paddle in gently, and the rest of the river hardly knew you were there. Until you fell in, of course.

"What's that?" she added suddenly, tipping her head sideways. "There's a dog in the water, I think." She remembered the glimpse of a

brownish-grey *something* she'd seen on her
very first day. This was the same colour – but it
definitely wasn't a fish.

"It doesn't look like a dog," Alfie said
uncertainly. "I can't see its ears."

Lissa scrunched her nose, frowning. "Yeah…
It's got to be, though. What else would be
swimming along here?"

The dog – or whatever it was –
seemed to have heard them
talking. It looked round
– just a little bump of
smooth rounded head
and two big dark
eyes. Then it ducked
under the surface
of the water and
disappeared.

Dad met Lissa on the bank at the end of the
paddleboarding session. At least he hadn't
forgotten about her. Alfie was standing next
to them, looking worried. It wasn't far to his
houseboat but Milli the instructor wouldn't
let him leave on his own, or go with Lissa and
Dad. She said she knew it seemed a bit fussy,
but it had to be the parent she had on the
paperwork who picked him up.

"Are you ready to go, Lissa?" Dad asked. He
was fidgeting, as though he wanted to get back
to work as soon as he could.

"No." Lissa turned to him, looking him in the eye as firmly as she could. Dad had already ruined their plans that morning. He could wait a bit. "No, can we wait with Alfie, please?"

Alfie gave an embarrassed sort of shrug. "You don't have to," he muttered.

Dad looked a bit surprised, Lissa thought, but he smiled at Alfie. "No problem." Lissa and Alfie helped Milli gather up the buoyancy aids and wetsuit boots and other odd bits, while Lissa's dad frowned at his phone. Lissa had wanted to tell him about that strange brownish-grey creature, to ask what he thought it might be – but Dad didn't look as though he'd be very interested.

"There's my mum!" Alfie said at last, his face clearing. He waved at a woman hurrying down the river path with a baby in a sling on her front.

"I'm so sorry!" she gasped to Milli when she got close enough. "Joshua was sick all over me just as I was setting off to get Alfie. I'm really sorry to keep you waiting."

Milli smiled. "Don't worry, it's fine. Thanks for helping, you two. Hope you enjoyed it. Just get in touch if you want to book again."

Lissa definitely wanted to do more paddleboarding, but it would be much better if Alfie was there too. She gave him a cautious, sideways look. What if she said she wanted to and he said he didn't? It had made things a lot more fun today, making a friend, but it would be awful if he'd thought she was really boring and couldn't wait to get away. But Alfie was nodding. She grinned at him and turned to Dad.

"Can I?"

"And me," Alfie said hopefully to his mum.

She looked flustered. "Oh! Yes, sure. Except I didn't bring my purse. I'll have to do it online." She jogged from foot to foot, trying to comfort Alfie's baby brother, who'd started grizzling.

"We've still got spaces on a not-quite-beginners class this time tomorrow," Milli suggested. "Now that you two know the basics."

"We can do tomorrow, can't we?" Alfie asked his mum.

"Yes... I think so. I'll sign you up later. We'd better go now though, Alfie, sorry. Joshua needs feeding again."

"See you tomorrow!" Lissa said, and Alfie grinned at her and waved as he and his mum hurried away.

"I'm sorry I couldn't make it," Dad said as they walked back to *Rose Dawn*. "It was good then?"

"Really good," Lissa agreed. She wondered for

a moment if Dad was going to suggest he came along tomorrow – she didn't know whether to be hopeful or not. But he still had work. And he probably wouldn't be able to come anyway, as he hadn't paddleboarded before. "You won't forget to book me in?"

"No, I promise. I'm sorry, Lissa. I didn't mean to forget about this morning."

"It's OK." Lissa smiled at him. "I had a great time. Alfie's nice, and we were really good at paddleboarding." She put her head on one side. "Way better than you would have been, Dad."

"Hey!"

The not-quite-beginners paddleboarding class started off in the same quiet backwater as Lissa and Alfie's first one, but the idea was to build up everyone's confidence so they could head out into the main stretch of the river. It was a bigger group today, and there were two instructors: Milli and a young man called Malhar.

"I hope we go past our houseboat," Alfie said, grinning excitedly as they paddled towards the main river. "And yours. I told my mum I'd try to wave at her if we did. She's going to look out for me."

Lissa nodded but she felt a bit sad. Dad would probably be inside, working. He wouldn't notice her waving. Although he said that sometimes he worked in the wheelhouse, under the canopy. She hadn't thought to warn him to watch for her, though. She knew he'd have liked to see her.

It was a bit nerve-wracking, venturing out into the open river. A long, thin rowing boat was shooting by, a team of eight rowers all striking the water fiercely in time. Behind it, a small powerboat was buzzing along with someone shouting at the rowers through a megaphone. Lissa definitely didn't want to get in their way. But Milli didn't look too worried. She beckoned everyone on and they splashed gently forward.

THE DAWN SEAL

Lissa could see passers-by on the path pointing at them, and she smiled to herself as she heard a younger girl asking if her family could do that too. She stood a little straighter on her board, trying to look cool and confident and not the slightest bit wobbly.

They were gliding slowly past Alfie's parents' houseboat – Alfie was waving his paddle at his mum, who was making baby Joshua wave back – when Lissa felt her paddleboard rock. She just about managed to keep her balance but her heart was thumping wildly. What had she done wrong? She'd been paddling the same as before. She hadn't moved suddenly or leaned over too much. She looked down at the water, feeling panicky. What if there was something down there? She'd been excited about seeing fish, but now her mind immediately went to sharks, and giant octopuses, or a massive crab... She knew it was a river, not the sea, but it didn't stop her imagining tentacles the size of tree trunks. Lissa let out a shaky breath. She'd probably just bumped into a shopping trolley. Milli had told them that people threw all sorts of silly things into the river and they had to watch out.

Then her board rocked again – and this time, Lissa saw why.

At the front of her paddleboard, a neat, domed head had popped out of the water, and two round dark eyes were gazing up at her. The creature had its paws on the board, smooth paws shining wet with river water and tipped with thick black claws.

Lissa stared at the creature silently. It was a seal – it had to be. She'd seen photos of them before, and when they'd gone to the seaside on holiday last year, Mickey had shown her seals while they were walking the path around a rocky bay. They'd been far away though, too far to see much more than dark greyish humps scattered along the rocks and the tideline.

She had never imagined being this close to a seal – Mickey had said they were shy and that the mums could be fierce protecting their cubs. It was best to watch them from a distance.

"Lissa…" Alfie had turned back from waving to his mum and Joshua, and now he was staring at Lissa and the seal. He looked awestruck. "What's that?"

"I think it's a seal," Lissa whispered back. She let out her breath in a silent squeak as the seal started to pull itself on to her paddleboard. It was tipping the board a little, unbalancing her, and she crouched down, then kneeled, and gripped the side of the board. What was she supposed to do? Should she jump off? Mickey had said that seals were fierce but Lissa wasn't scared of this one. Shocked, definitely, but not scared.

The seal looked pretty surprised too. Perhaps it hadn't expected anyone to be on the board.

"What are you doing?" Lissa whispered. "Are you OK?" If what Mickey had said about seals being shy was right, did it mean there was something wrong with this one?

The seal heaved itself further out of the water and Lissa stifled a giggle. It looked just like her and Alfie the day before, the first time they'd tried to get back on the paddleboards. Except the seal was a lot better at it. It flopped heavily on to the end of Lissa's board and seemed to sigh with relief. Its dark eyes looked mournful, she thought. But perhaps that was just the shape seals' eyes always were. This seal was definitely weary though. She could hear it breathing hard and it was slumped on the

board as though it had been desperate for
a rest.

Lissa crouched there watching and Alfie
paddled a little closer. "Wow," he whispered.
"Lissa, you're so lucky."

"I know. I think this is what we saw
yesterday, do you remember? When we
thought there was a dog in the water? It had
spots, like this seal."

"Yeah... But what's it doing here?"

"I don't know." Lissa gave a tiny shrug. She
didn't know, but she couldn't help feeling
that the seal had climbed on to her board
for a reason. Perhaps it knew that she was
sad and worried too – that she'd understand
it needed help.

"Hey! Look!"

One of the boys in the paddleboarding

group had spotted the seal. He was so surprised that he dropped his paddle and nearly fell off his board as he tried to grab it back.

Everyone else stopped paddling to look over their shoulders and Milli scudded quickly back to Lissa and Alfie.

"Are you OK, Lissa?" she called quietly. "Don't be scared."

"I'm not," Lissa murmured back. How could she be scared of the seal when it needed her?

"OK. Just keep still. I've seen this happen a couple of times before, but usually much further down the river. The seals hop on to the paddleboards for a rest. Give it a few minutes and it'll go back into the water itself."

"I don't mind," Lissa said. She didn't want the seal to go.

"Can we stroke it?" called another of the paddleboarders, a woman who'd come with her daughter.

"No," Milli said firmly. "In fact, can you

all move back a bit, please? Malhar will take the rest of the group on for the minute and I'll stay with Lissa."

"And me!" Alfie said.

"Yes, OK, and you, Alfie. Please, everyone."

"It doesn't look dangerous," the woman argued, coming closer.

"It's so cute," her daughter agreed. "Can I get a selfie with it? Can I get on your board?" she asked Lissa.

Lissa shook her head, horrified. The seal was exhausted and frightened as it was. How could the girl even think about climbing on to her board? That would definitely scare it more. The seal was already watching the girl and fidgeting anxiously. It was probably deciding if it should get back in the water.

Milli paddled between the girl and Lissa.

"You can't touch the seal, it's a young one and it's probably really scared, which might make it bite you."

The woman and her daughter looked doubtful but they paddled a little further away.

"Thanks," Lissa whispered. "I'd be scared if all these people were crowding round me too."

Milli smiled at her. "Just stay still and let it be. You're doing great, Lissa, don't worry."

"I thought seals lived in the sea," Alfie said quietly to Milli. He was kneeling on his board now too, watching just as eagerly as Lissa.

"Yeah," Milli agreed. "They do. But the River Thames joins on to the sea, remember? Lots of seals live further downstream, where the river and the sea meet. Sometimes they swim upriver. Not often, but sometimes. Usually it's young ones who've got a bit confused." She frowned. "I hope this little one's OK."

"What do you mean?" Lissa asked anxiously. She'd thought the seal looked tired and sad, and now it seemed that Milli did too.

"Well, it's like I said. They don't usually come up this far, and sometimes they get confused by the locks and they can get trapped upriver. This one looks a bit thin, like it's been stuck here a while."

"What, they can't get round the locks?" Alfie asked.

Lissa eyed the seal. She still found the locks a bit confusing, even though Dad had tried to explain them a few times. Locks were for when a river or a canal was on a slope – they helped level out the water, a bit like a step up or down, so a boat could continue on its way. A seal wouldn't know how they worked. It would just see the big gates blocking the river. It would probably be really frightened.

"Hey, I think it's moving," Lissa murmured to Milli and Alfie. The seal was shifting on the end of the board, wriggling about and peering at the water. It glanced quickly back at Lissa and she caught her breath at those sad dark eyes. Then it was gone, swimming swiftly downstream, back towards the water sports centre and the little island.

Alfie's mum had to hurry away with him after the paddleboarding session – she needed to take baby Joshua for an appointment – so Lissa was left waiting with Milli.

"Sorry," she muttered. "He'll be here in a minute." Alfie's mum yesterday, her dad today – it was so embarrassing.

"I know he will, don't worry," Milli said. She was so nice, Lissa thought. "You'll have to tell him about the seal! Malhar got a photo of it – he's a lot braver than me. I hate getting my phone out when we're on the water, I always think I'm going to drop it, even though it's got a special case. We'll email it to your dad."

"Where do you think the seal's gone now?" Lissa asked. She couldn't help thinking that the seal had wanted her to help it, even though she knew that was silly. It was probably just luck that the seal had chosen her board to climb on. But still...

Milli looked thoughtful.

"I'm not sure, but I wonder if it was making for the island?" She pointed at the wooded patch in the middle of the river. "It swam off in that direction, didn't it? It would be a good place to get out of the water easily. One of the reasons seals end up sitting on people's boards is that it's hard for them to climb out of the river, with boats and concrete walls all along the banks. They need a bit of a slope."

Lissa nodded. That made sense. With no back legs, seals wouldn't be able to push themselves up. She wasn't sure they'd even be able to get up the steps she'd seen here and there along the river path. And the island was deserted – like Alfie had said, it was too small for anyone to live on, or even visit for a picnic. It would be a perfect seal hideout.

"Did you say you thought it's a young seal?" she asked. She'd seen photos of fluffy white seal babies, but perhaps this one was in between, not quite a baby and not an adult. The same sort of age as her, almost.

"I don't know that much about them, but there was something on the news a while ago," Milli said slowly. "I'm sure it said it was the young seals that get confused and come too far up the river. Pups, they're called, when they're little."

Pups! Lissa smiled to herself. It was such a cute word, and actually the seal did seem like a pup – those big dark eyes were a bit like a dog's. Instead of just saying "the seal" to herself, Lissa decided, she would call it Pup. It was the perfect name.

She wondered if she would see Pup again...

"I hope the seal's all right," Milli murmured. "It did look a bit thin. I thought seals were rounder than that..."

"Maybe we should feed it?" Lissa suggested. She didn't really know how. What food could she get for a seal? Would it like a tin of tuna?

"Maybe... And I think I saw something about registering when you'd spotted them. I'll have a look online tonight."

"I will too," Lissa said, nodding excitedly. "I bet Dad can help me."

"Oh, there he is now, look. Isn't that your dad? You can ask him." Milli pointed up the path and Lissa swung round, excited to tell him her news.

"Dad, guess what we saw—"

But Dad wasn't listening. "Not now, Liss, I'm supposed to be in a meeting." He was practically turning back down the path before he'd seen she was following him. And he didn't apologize to Milli for being late picking her up. Lissa flushed scarlet. The meeting was more important than she was – and now Milli knew it too.

"I'm sorry," she muttered to Milli and then hurried down the path after him, trailing her towel and almost in tears.

"You look a bit upset, Lissa, are you all right?"
Lissa looked up from the book she'd been
pretending to read in the wheelhouse and saw
Rosy smiling at her from the path. She was on
her own today, without her grumpy bulldog.

Lissa didn't really know what to say. No,
she wasn't all right. She was miserable and
lonely and disappointed and hurt. And a
lot of other things. But she also didn't want
to start spilling her feelings to someone
she didn't know that well. Alfie had been
different, since he was feeling abandoned
too. Talking to him had made things a lot
better – Lissa was lucky that Mum and
Mickey had tried so hard to make her feel
special when Zoe was born.

"I'm fine," she said to Rosy, blinking away
the tears that were threatening to spill over.
It was always the same, whenever she was
upset and someone was nice to her, it just
made her want to cry.

Rosy looked at her for a moment, with a little crease over the top of her nose. Then she seemed to decide she was going to take Lissa's word for it. She smiled and lifted up the pair of binoculars on a strap around her neck, showing them to Lissa. "I'm going bird watching," she explained. "Very soothing, you should try it. I'd be happy to take you with me one day, if your dad agrees."

Lissa nodded politely. She didn't feel enthusiastic about bird watching just then, but that was probably because she was miserable about Dad, and worried about the seal. She didn't want to hurt Rosy's feelings though. She got up and came to lean over the door to the wheelhouse, so she could talk to her better. "When you've been bird watching, have you ever seen other things?"

"Such as?" Rosy put her head on one side.

"We saw a seal! In my paddleboarding class this morning. It actually climbed on the end of my board and sat there for ages."

"Oh my, lucky you to get so close." Rosy beamed at her. "That's exciting!"

Lissa nodded, trying to smile. That's exactly what she'd wanted Dad to say. She hadn't even told him about the seal. As soon as they'd got back on board *Rose Dawn*, he'd disappeared off to his meeting.

"Do you know anything about seals?" If Rosy was into bird watching and wildlife, maybe she would be able to help.

"Not a huge amount," Rosy said slowly. "I have spotted them along here before – there was one a couple of days ago, close to the little island. I wonder if it's the same one you saw. I was just looking out over the stern of my boat and there was a seal swimming by! It stared back at me too. I think it was just as curious about me as I was about it. I love their whiskers – they reminded me of a cat."

Lissa nodded. Rosy was right. Pup had looked a tiny bit like a cat, with the same curved muzzle and full bunches of whiskers. Pup even had spiky white eyebrow whiskers like a cat too. But the eyes were completely different.

"Seals aren't the most unusual creatures people see swimming up the river, you know," Rosy went on, gazing out at the water as though she might see something strange and exciting at any moment. Lissa couldn't help turning to look too. "There have been lots of sightings of dolphins in the Thames, and even whales!"

"But … but they'd never fit! Whales are

huge!" Lissa said disbelievingly.

"Yes, they are, but I promise it's true. And you're right, the river just isn't deep enough for them. They're used to the open sea and the Thames is only about five metres deep at the most." Rosy sighed. "The minke whale that got stuck in the river last year died, I'm afraid, even though rescuers tried so hard to save it. I remember being excited to see a whale at first, and then we began to realize that it was ill and it wasn't going to survive. It was desperately sad."

Lissa swallowed hard. Rosy's story *was* sad – and it made her remember what Milli had said about the seal looking thin.

"Milli, she's the paddleboarding instructor, she thought the seal was a young one, and maybe not very good at feeding itself. I suppose that means fishing?" Lissa added uncertainly.

"She said maybe there was somewhere we were supposed to report seeing a seal. Perhaps someone ought to be helping it, like they tried to help the whale."

"Yes, London Zoo tracks seal sightings," Rosy agreed. "I can do that for you, if you like. I reported the one I saw the other day. I suppose the seal could be stuck on this stretch of the river."

"Because of the lock?" Lissa asked. "Milli said that too. That the seal might not be able to get back downriver again."

"Mmmm. If the seal is actually trapped, I'm sure the team of divers who came to help with the whale would try to rescue it. But we'd need to be sure it was in trouble before we called them out." Rosy smiled. "The seal's probably fine. Just enjoying our bit of the river! I know that Phil – he's the lock keeper – he's let seals out of the lock before. I remember him telling me about it. We should definitely keep an eye out for this one though, especially if it's only a pup."

"OK." Lissa nodded. That sounded hopeful. Maybe Pup was all right after all. "It would be great if you could log the sighting with the zoo. I want to look seals up anyway, though. Dad said I could use his old laptop while I was staying."

It had felt so special to have Pup sit there on the end of her board, gazing at her – but the little seal had looked lost. Lost and frightened. Rosy was probably right, and there was nothing to worry about, but Lissa still couldn't help thinking that Pup had been asking her for help.

Over the next few days, Lissa set to work
to find out everything she could about
seals – and particularly seals in the River
Thames. She borrowed Dad's old laptop for
research online. He was happy to let her use
it. Actually, she thought it made him feel a
bit less guilty – he was still working on his
unexpected project, although he did promise
it would soon be finished.

Lissa even discovered that the Wi-Fi Dad
had set up inside *Rose Dawn* stretched up as
far as the barge's roof, which was a perfect

89

sunbathing and river-watching spot. She had
to be a bit careful getting the laptop up there,
putting it on her back in a special rucksack
case, but then she had her own private
camping spot.

Lissa was pretty sure Mum would have said
no – there were no railings or any sort of edge
to stop her falling off. But Dad just muttered
something about it perhaps being sensible to
wear her buoyancy aid up there, just in case,
and that it was absolutely vital not to drop the
laptop in the river – which Lissa had worked
out for herself – and then let her get on with it.

She didn't wear the buoyancy aid, not after
the first couple of hours. It was too hot and
it got in the way. She used it as a cushion for
her elbows when she was lying on her front
looking at the laptop instead. Up there, on

top of the roof, she had a brilliant view along the river – she alternated her research with gazing at the water, looking hopefully for Pup. She was pretty sure she'd seen lots of fish, just flashes of silver in the water, but no seals.

Lissa found quite a few news stories online about seals swimming up the river. There were lots of articles about the minke whale that Rosy had mentioned as well. She had almost not believed Rosy's story about the whale, but it was definitely true, and it was really sad. Some of the stories about seals were pretty worrying too.

Lissa reckoned that Pup was probably a common seal. She hadn't even known there were two sorts of seals that lived around the British coast. The other kind were called grey seals, and they were bigger – although that didn't help much as she didn't have another seal to compare Pup with.

Apparently, the best way to tell was by looking at their noses, and she had stared at Pup's nose for a while on the paddleboard.

Common seals had noses that were much closer to their eyes than grey seals, and their nostrils made a V shape, while grey seals' nostrils were parallel lines. Common seals had short, rounded heads, and looking at the photos that Malhar had taken and Milli had emailed to Dad, Lissa was pretty sure that's what Pup was.

The funny thing was that common seals weren't actually common at all. In Britain they were rarer than grey seals. Lissa had started making notes in a little notebook that Mum had given her because there was so much to remember. Common seals liked to lie with their tails lifted up. There were lots of photos of them lying on the shore, curled up like bananas. Lissa thought they looked really sweet.

But if she was right about Pup being a common seal, it meant Pup might be only a month old. The websites Lissa had been looking at said that common seals gave birth to their babies in June or July. The pups were born with brown or greyish fur like their parents, and they could swim and dive with their mothers almost as soon as they were born. The mothers would feed them on their milk for three to four weeks, but after that the seal pups had to look after themselves, starting by feeding on small food like shrimps. Lissa had watched her mum eating prawns in a restaurant, taking the shells off bit by bit. It looked horrible and fiddly and she hadn't wanted to try one, even when Mum offered to shell it for her. She couldn't imagine crunchy, whiskery prawns being the first solid food that seal pups got to eat.

Once they'd got used to shrimps, the pups would move on to catching fish instead, and they'd learn by watching the adult seals – no one actually taught them how to do it. Lissa was starting to feel really sorry for the pups. Imagine being that young and left to fend for themselves! One of the websites had said that only half of common seal pups actually survived to be fully grown. She wasn't that surprised, but it made her more worried about Pup than ever.

"You look comfy up there!"

Lissa glanced over and saw Rosy waving at her from the river path.

"I'm finding out about seals!" she called back. "And watching for our seal again – but

I haven't seen her."

Rosy nodded thoughtfully. "Well, I hope you do. It makes me so happy, thinking about the wild creatures living all around us. It isn't that long since the River Thames was declared dead, did you know? It was so polluted, biologists said nothing could possibly live in it. That was back in the 1950s. Things have changed so much since then."

Lissa glanced at the glittering water and nodded. "It's beautiful now. I love it here."

Rosy smiled at her. "Would you like to borrow my old binoculars?" she suggested. "They might help you spot the seal."

Lissa wasn't entirely sure how binoculars worked and whether they'd help, but she said yes anyway. She liked Rosy, and someone who knew so much about wildlife and the river was probably right. "Yes, please!" she said.

"I'll pop back and get them for you now. If I leave it till later on, I'll never remember." She marched briskly back down the path to her own boat and Lissa watched, feeling a bit guilty. But it didn't take long for Rosy to return, climbing up on to *Rose Dawn*'s side with a brown leather case slung round her neck. "Here you go," she told Lissa, passing the case over.

"They look precious," Lissa said doubtfully. What if she broke them?

"It's only my old pair," Rosy reassured her. "My son gave me some snazzy new ones last Christmas. Open the case, have a look."

Lissa undid the buckle and lifted out a pair of heavy black binoculars – they looked a bit like two little telescopes stuck together.

"Now look through them. You can turn the little wheel on that side to help get a sharper view."

"Oh wow…" Lissa lifted the binoculars to her eyes and gasped as the river seemed to jump towards her, the trees on the opposite bank suddenly a mass of separate, shimmering leaves. She pointed the binoculars down at a swan swimming by and she could see each of its crisp feathers. "They're amazing!" she told Rosy admiringly. "Thank you! Are you sure it's OK for me to borrow them?"

"Of course. I'm just really glad to see someone your age interested in wildlife. Enjoy them. Let me know if you see the seal again!"

Lissa sat cross-legged on the roof,

practising with the binoculars. She could see
so much – there was a bird's nest in one of
the trees across the river, she was sure…

"Hey!"

Lissa peered down at the river path through the binoculars and saw an enormous Alfie looking up at her enviously.

"Mum said I could come and see if you were in, and if you wanted to come over to ours. I wish I'd asked if I could come over here instead, though – we can't sit on the roof of our houseboat. I'm really jealous."

Lissa smiled, hoping she didn't look too smug. "You can come up here another time," she suggested. "If your mum and dad let you."

Alfie eyed her thoughtfully. "Yeah, actually, I think my mum might not be sure…"

"Mine too." Lissa sighed. "But I'd love to come to yours. Is it OK if I bring these? Rosy lent them to me. You know, she lives close to you and she has the bulldog? I just have to ask my dad though."

Lissa's dad looked delighted when she asked if it was OK to go to Alfie's. "That would be great, Liss. I'm really sorry I haven't spent much time with you these past few days. Let me go and find something you can take to give to Alfie's mum. I reckon there's some cake bars in the galley. Hang on."

He insisted on walking Lissa and Alfie back to Alfie's houseboat too, even though Alfie assured him they wouldn't get lost.

"Dad, it's straight down the river path from one boat to the other!"

"I know. But I want to say thank you to Alfie's mum for letting you come over and I'll give her my number, just in case."

Lissa and Alfie sighed at each other, and while they hurried ahead of Dad, Lissa told him all the things she'd found out about seals.

"I'm worried about Pup. Apparently, if they come out of the water really close to people, like on a beach next to someone having a picnic, it's because they're running out of energy. Well, climbing on a paddleboard, that's even worse than a beach with people, isn't it?"

"Definitely," Alfie agreed.

"But we did the right thing not scaring her back into the water."

"Her? Did you find out she's a girl, then?"

Lissa shook her head. "No... But saying *it* just felt weird. So I decided Pup's a her."

"OK." Alfie shrugged. "What did you mean about not scaring her back in?"

"I read that if you do that it uses up even

more of their energy and it can make life even harder for them. If they're worn out you have to give them time to recover." Lissa looked at Alfie worriedly. "I hope she found somewhere to go and have a proper rest."

Once Dad had exchanged numbers with Alfie's mum, Lissa and Alfie settled on the little deck at the front of the boat, taking turns to look through the binoculars and eating snacks that Alfie's mum had given them.

"There's something over there," Alfie mumbled, with his mouth full of banana. "Look. Maybe it's Pup, Lissa!"

Lissa turned the binoculars over to the other bank – there was definitely something… She sighed. "Alfie, it's a plastic bag!"

"It doesn't look like one," Alfie muttered. "Can I have a go with them?"

THE DAWN SEAL

The plastic bag was their only spot that afternoon, apart from ducks. Perhaps everything was fine and Pup had gone back through the lock on her own. Maybe she did it all the time, and she waited for the lock keeper to open the gates for her? Lissa could only hope she was right.

The next morning Lissa woke up way before she usually did. She wasn't sure why – and normally she'd have looked at her watch, groaned and turned over to go back to sleep. But not this morning. Lissa felt … twitchy. She wanted to be up and out by the river, she realized, leaning down from her bunk to peer out of the porthole. It was only just getting light and she could see mist wreathing all along the water, faintly streaked with pink.

It looks like the perfect time for a shy young seal to be out, Lissa thought. When she'd looked for Pup over the last few days, there had always been people tramping loudly up and down the river path, and boats going by. Was it any wonder the seal hadn't shown herself? Lissa dropped down out of her bunk and threw her clothes on in a hurry. Then she grabbed Rosy's binoculars, before slipping out to the wheelhouse, and then the bank.

The drifting mist made the river look so different – the boats either side of *Rose Dawn* seemed to be far away, floating in a magical watery world. Lissa climbed up carefully on to the barge roof again, glad of the grip on her trainers – the roof was slippery with dew. She sat there, hugging her knees tightly and shivering a little. It would probably be hot later but the morning was chilly. Lissa didn't mind. She felt as though she was the only person on the river – she was so lucky.

There was a faint splash at *Rose Dawn*'s

stern and Lissa looked round hopefully.

Pup was there, gazing back at her through the fading trails of mist.

"Hey…" Lissa drew in a breath, and then whispered, "Are you OK? I've been looking for you."

The seal swam a little closer, looking curiously up at Lissa on the roof of the boat. She didn't seem too worried that a human was there in her peaceful misty dawn. She watched Lissa for a moment more and then dived under the surface of the water. Lissa guessed Pup was fishing. That was good. She couldn't be scared of Lissa if she was just carrying on looking for her breakfast, could she?

Lissa remembered the binoculars and took them out of the case, ready to get a close-up view of Pup if she surfaced again. *There!* A small, spotted grey head had popped up, further into the middle of the river. Hurriedly, Lissa focused her binoculars and smiled to herself as Pup's little face leaped out at her. She really did look a lot like a cat – just without any ears. A beautiful, spotted tabby cat…

THE DAWN SEAL

Lissa watched for a good ten minutes as Pup dived and surfaced with hardly a splash – and then one of the super-thin rowing boats came shooting by, out for an early morning practice. Pup watched it cautiously and decided it was time to go. She headed away up the river towards Alfie's houseboat and the little island.

"Maybe we were right?" Lissa wondered out loud. "That's where you're staying." It was a perfect hideout – she and Milli had thought so the first time they saw Pup. Lissa imagined her wriggling on to the muddy bank under the willow trees, her spotted coat camouflaging her perfectly in the dappled sunlight.

After that, Lissa found herself waking up early every morning, just after dawn, so she was ready to watch out for Pup. She almost always saw her, even if it was only for a moment or two before the sun rose higher and burned away the river mist. It was their special time together.

6

"Lissa? Do you want some breakfast?"

Lissa blinked sleepily down at Dad. He was standing in the doorway, smiling at her. Then she gasped and sat up – almost banging her head on the cabin ceiling.

"Hey, careful!"

"What time is it?" Lissa asked urgently, clambering out of her bunk.

"Um, about half past nine? It's OK, there's nothing special to be up for. I guessed you were probably tired out after yesterday, so I let you sleep."

Nothing to be up for! Lissa sighed. Dad just didn't understand. It was the second day running she'd missed seeing Pup. Dad had nearly finished his work project, which meant he was feeling a lot less stressed. He wanted them to catch up on all the fun day trips he'd promised at the beginning of the holidays. Yesterday he'd looked at her list and they'd gone to visit the Tower of London. Lissa had wanted to go there for ages, and it *was* amazing – but when she'd found herself by Traitors' Gate, where the boats would come to take prisoners to be executed, she wasn't thinking about Anne Boleyn or anyone else from history. She was looking at the water and wondering if she might see a seal swimming by...

When she'd first come to stay on the barge,

Lissa had been really looking forward to hanging out with Dad. It was supposed to be their time together, after all those weeks of not seeing him. Maybe that day at the Tower of London and the other trips Dad was planning would make up for the time he'd spent working. But now Lissa realized she hadn't wanted the day trips all that much. She'd wanted everyday things. Playing games and watching TV together. She'd just wanted Dad to be around.

He hadn't even talked to Lissa about ideas for her birthday, and that was only two days away! Lissa wanted so much to ask Dad if he had a plan, but at the same time she couldn't bear to. What if he'd forgotten her birthday? She was going to be ten – double figures. It felt like it should be special.

If she'd been at home, Mum would have had a massive long list of birthday plans, probably colour-coded. They were more than two weeks into the holidays now and Lissa was really, really missing Mum and Zoe. A phone call every day wasn't the same as seeing them.

Why wouldn't Dad talk to her? Mum talked to her about Pup more than Dad did, and she wasn't even there!

Yesterday the little seal hadn't appeared when Lissa went to look for her at dawn – Lissa had no idea why. But she'd been really hoping to spot her this morning. She should have known how tired she'd be after their day out and set an alarm.

Perhaps she could ask Rosy and Alfie if they'd seen Pup, Lissa thought as she got dressed. She could ask Dad to keep watch for her too, she supposed. But there didn't seem to be a lot of point in that, and Lissa wanted to see Pup herself. She missed her. Watching for Pup had filled the gaps when Dad was busy working – but it was more than that. She'd filled up the hole Lissa felt inside, when Dad didn't listen to her, or when his work seemed more important. Lissa was just as lonely and out of place as Pup was.

"Perhaps Pup's gone back down the river? To where all the rest of the seals are?" Lissa suggested to Rosy. They were both on the path by *Rose Dawn* and Lissa was making a fuss of Jack, who seemed to have got used to her now. He almost looked as if he might be pleased to see her, although it was a bit hard to tell with all those wrinkles.

Rosy sucked her teeth worriedly. "Maybe. But I was talking to a friend yesterday, and she said she'd seen a seal beached on those concrete steps downriver a bit, do you know where I mean? Just before the lock?"

Lissa shook her head.

"It's not that far, so I suppose it must have been your Pup. I can't imagine there are two young seals this far up the river. I wonder if she was trying to work out how to get past the lock, poor little thing."

"Did your friend say if the seal was freckly?" Lissa burst out. "Pup is, she's sort of spotted all over."

"No, she didn't, Lissa, sorry. But she said this one wasn't looking too good. Apparently she's seen them before, and she thought this one looked very small and thin."

"Oh…" Lissa frowned worriedly. "I've been seeing Pup early in the mornings. I thought she looked OK. But I haven't seen her for the last couple of days. I was out with Dad yesterday, we went to the Tower of London.

I didn't wake up in time to look for her today, I was really tired…"

"Don't panic." Rosy patted her arm. "My friend called the hotline for the diver rescue team. They told her to monitor the seal, but they know about Pup now, and if they need to come and rescue her, they will."

"But why don't they just come anyway?"

Rosy sighed. "Apparently they get more than two thousand calls a year, and they're all volunteers. They can't be everywhere. But also it's quite difficult to trap seals, and it can be stressful for them too. So if the seals can make it back to safety by themselves, it's better for everyone."

Lissa swallowed. "Did you know only half of common seal pups grow up to be adults?" she asked Rosy quietly.

"Is it that few? No, I didn't know. Oh dear. Well, I suppose all we can do is keep an eye out, Lissa. If we spot Pup in difficulties, we can call the rescue team again."

Lissa nodded determinedly. She wasn't going to let anything happen to Pup.

"Time for dinner, Liss. You'd better come down off there, you've been up on the roof all day." Dad was standing on the gunwale, the rim that ran around the edge of the barge, looking up at her.

Lissa was about to argue, when she realized Dad was right. She *had* been up there all day, watching for Pup through Rosy's binoculars. She still hadn't seen her, and it was a whole day since Rosy had told

her about the seal on the concrete steps.
Lissa was getting more and more worried.

"I never expected you to be so interested in wildlife," Dad said.

Lissa shrugged. "It's not just any wildlife. It's Pup."

"Pup?" Dad sounded vague. "Oh, the seal. Have you seen it again, then?"

Lissa shook her head, feeling frustrated. "Not for three whole days. I'm really worried about her." She scrambled down on to the gunwale and followed Dad back along the bank to the wheelhouse and indoors. "Dad, can we go for a walk this evening to look for her?"

Dad was getting pans out of the cupboard and looking for the pasta. Lissa wasn't sure he was listening very hard. "Why?"

"Because I haven't seen her for three days, and I'm worried," Lissa said, trying to be patient.

"But isn't that a good thing? I thought it was better for seals to be out at sea? Or at least further down the river in the estuary?" The estuary was the bit of the Thames where it joined the sea. It was where most of the seals in the river lived.

"Yes… But this seal's been around our bit of the river for a while now," Lissa tried to explain. "Lots of people have spotted her, and she's very young and too thin. And now she's disappeared! Don't you see, Dad? I'm really worried! If there's something wrong, we have to call the diver team to come and rescue her!"

Dad looked up and smiled sympathetically at her. "I'm sure the seal will be fine, Lissie. You don't need to worry. It isn't up to you to look after her, is it?"

Lissa stared at him, speechless – and then she was furious. How could Dad say that? Maybe it wasn't her job to look after Pup, but that didn't mean she couldn't care! Pup

was a wild creature and she was in danger.
Lissa couldn't just hope that someone else
would sort it out.

"I'll go on my own, then, if you're too
busy!" she said angrily.

"Hey…" Her dad turned round, staring at
her in surprise. "Don't be silly. Of course you're
not going off on your own. And what was that
about, anyway? Who said I was too busy?"

"You're too busy for everything!" Lissa
shouted, her voice tangled up with tears.
"You don't care about me at all!" She didn't
know if she was angry about Pup, or her
birthday or Dad's stupid work project. It
had all mixed up into one huge unfairness.
"I don't want any dinner!" she yelled at him,
and she stomped away to her cabin. She
couldn't even slam the stupid sliding door.

It was the morning after Lissa's fight with
Dad and she still hadn't spoken to him. He'd
tried to talk to her when she grumped into the
galley to grab some cereal, but Lissa had stared
into her bowl and stayed silent and eventually
Dad had given up and put on the radio.

Alfie had turned up outside *Rose Dawn* after
breakfast – he did that most days now. Lissa
really liked having him living so close. They
were sitting on the grass at the edge of the
mooring and Alfie was picking at it, wrapping
it around one finger. He was trying to avoid
looking at Lissa, she could tell. He was
embarrassed. Not as embarrassed as she was,
but still. Lissa hadn't meant to tell Alfie what
had happened with Dad, but then she hadn't

been able to keep it all bottled up either.

"I don't think your dad meant it like that," he said quietly. "Like Pup didn't matter."

"It sounded like he did," Lissa mumbled. "And I don't get it – who does he think is going to look after Pup if I don't? Someone has to watch out for her and I think it should be me!" She looked up at Alfie, frowning. "What if Pup's ill? She could be starving if she's not been able to catch enough fish. I'm going to look for her."

"I thought your dad said you couldn't?"

"I don't care," Lissa said stubbornly. "And he probably won't notice anyway. He's spent the last two weeks working." She paused a moment, trying to be fair. "Well, he did take me out for the day, to the Tower of London. And I know he has to work because he needs the money. But he promised the summer wouldn't be like this. He told Mum he'd be around all the time, doing stuff with me, and he just isn't." Lissa sighed. "The thing is, I think Pup might be on the island. I wish I was old enough to hire one of the paddleboards from the water sports centre, then I could go and look for her. I know I can't rescue her on my own, but at least if we could find out where she is we could call the diver rescue team and tell them."

Alfie was silent. Then after a while he nodded decisively. "I'll come with you to the island. We can use Dad's canoe. When shall we go?"

Lissa woke up in the dark with a jump and silenced the alarm on her watch, her heart thudding fast. She was pretty sure Dad's cabin was too far away for him to have heard it, but she was going to have to be careful. She'd put her pyjamas on before going to bed, even though she was planning to sneak out so early it was practically the middle of the night. She still wasn't talking to Dad, but she knew he'd come and check on her before he went to sleep. Everything had to look normal.

She slipped carefully out of her top bunk,

half hanging from the ladder to try to stop it creaking. Then she dressed in her warmest clothes. It was the middle of summer but Lissa knew it would be really cold this early in the morning.

Lissa grabbed her waterproof jacket and her torch, and slid open the door, centimetre by centimetre. Then she crept up the little passageway to the steps and the wheelhouse, telling herself there was only a couple of hours' difference. It was just like her early morning moments with Pup.

Except that it wasn't.

The night was strangely bright, lit by the street lamps that ran along the side of the river path. The lamplight seemed to have bleached the colour out of everything and the shadows were long, eerie lines of darkness. It was horrible and Lissa couldn't make herself walk out into it.

"You have to," she whispered fiercely. "Alfie's waiting for you! We have to help Pup!" She thought of those dark, worried eyes gazing at her from the end of her paddleboard and made herself step forwards.

Shaking, she edged out on to the gunwale and jumped down to the path. Then she set off, hurrying along to Alfie's houseboat. Dad was going to be furious when he found out what she'd done. She wasn't supposed to go out on her own at all, especially not in the dark. And now she was disappearing off down the path, without even telling Dad. But she didn't have a choice.

Lissa scurried on, trying not to imagine strange figures lurking in the puddles of shadow among the bushes, and footsteps in the sound of her own panicked breathing.

"Hey!"

Lissa jumped so sharply she almost fell backwards.

"It's me!" Alfie hissed from down below in the river, in the canoe. "Don't jump like that, you'll fall in. And shh!"

He sounded nervous too and that made Lissa feel better. "I wasn't saying anything!" she breathed back. "Wow – you got the canoe!"

"I said I would, didn't I?" Alfie was looking up at her, his face a pale blur against the dark, shining water. Alfie's dad had a big, open canoe and he'd taught Alfie to paddle it. The canoe was usually tied up at the side of their houseboat under a waterproof cover.

There was no way Alfie's parents would

let him and Lissa borrow it, which was why
they were meeting just before dawn. Alfie
had said his mum and dad were so tired with
Joshua waking them up all the time that he
reckoned he could get the canoe without them
noticing, so long as Joshua didn't start crying
unexpectedly and wake everyone up.

Lissa had seen at once that it was a brilliant
idea. With the canoe, they could easily get
to the island. Whenever Lissa had seen Pup,
the little seal had always headed off in that
direction. Milli had said it was the perfect place
for a seal to haul out and rest. It was where Lissa
and Alfie had first seen her too, when they'd
thought that she was a dog swimming in the
river. It made sense that she would be there.
They just had to be brave enough to go.

"Your little brother didn't wake up, then?"

Lissa whispered, crouching on the edge of
the bank.

"No, I timed it right – he usually falls back
to sleep around now. I'm going to go along
to the jetty just past *Rose Dawn*, then you
can climb in, OK?"

Lissa nodded, hurrying along the bank as
Alfie glided swiftly beside her. She could hear
the splash of his paddle in the quiet night.
Everything seemed much less frightening now
she wasn't alone.

Alfie had already drawn up by the jetty when
Lissa reached it and he was clinging to one of
the posts. "Here, have this." He passed her a
buoyancy aid and Lissa zipped it up over her
waterproof. Then she sat down on the edge of
the jetty and wriggled her feet out to step in.
The canoe seemed to twist underneath her, and

she tried not to squeak as she clambered inside.
There were people sleeping all around them.
They couldn't get caught now.

"All right?" Alfie handed her a paddle and Lissa nodded.

"It's still really dark out on the water, though. I can't see where we're going."

"I know." Alfie hesitated a moment. "But … it's like you said about the path the other day, isn't it? It's not like we can get lost. There's only one river and the island's in the middle somewhere…"

Lissa laughed weakly. "Yeah … we just have to hope we hit it…"

"I'm going to push off," Alfie told her. "Ready?"

"Uh-huh." Lissa wasn't but she didn't think there was any point in waiting.

The dark water lifted the canoe gently and Lissa could feel it pulling at her paddle. They were on their way to find Pup. A little thread of hope wound itself around her middle and she drew in a deeper breath, the first since her alarm had jolted her out of sleep.

"I can't see if we're close to the island," she whispered to Alfie a few moments later.

"We won't miss it…" Alfie said, but she could hear the worry in his voice.

"What if you paddle and I turn my torch on?" Lissa suggested. "Like a searchlight? It's a good torch, really bright. We'd spot the island then."

"OK." Alfie reached back and took Lissa's paddle, stowing it down the side of the canoe, and Lissa worked the torch out of her jacket pocket under the buoyancy aid and pressed the switch. A thin beam of silvery light floated out across the water, cutting the darkness ahead.

"Yeah, that's better." Alfie nodded. "We're nearly there, I think."

He paddled on and Lissa crouched behind him, swinging the torch beam slowly across the river.

"There!" she said at last. The torchlight had caught a fringe of drooping willow branches – the island was already slipping past them in the darkness.

Alfie gasped, driving the paddle down hard to turn them in towards the island, and Lissa reached out to catch at the willows as they came in close.

"We did it!" They cheered each other in whispered hisses, shushing and laughing. Then Alfie stepped cautiously out on to the muddy slope and Lissa hopped out after him, feeling the mud suck and swallow at her plimsolls. They pulled the canoe up the slope, beaching her securely out of the water.

Alfie pulled out his own torch and they cast their lights across the island, hoping to see a small, spotted seal staring back at them. But there was nothing – only faint rustles from several sleepy and affronted ducks.

They shuffled and rattled their wings as the torchlight passed over them, and then tucked their heads away in their feathers, like Lissa hiding under the duvet when she didn't want to get up.

"We should pull the canoe up a bit further," Lissa suggested. "Then we can walk round the island and look for Pup." But her torch beam looked thin against the tangles of trailing undergrowth, and she hesitated. Those eerie puddles of shadow were back. She didn't want to set out across the island in the dark.

"Ummm." Alfie swung his torch round too, and then they looked at each other. "It won't be that long till it's light," he suggested.

"You want to wait until morning?" Lissa said, trying not to sound too hopeful, in case

THE DAWN SEAL

Alfie thought she wasn't brave enough for their adventure.

"You always saw her at dawn, didn't you? Maybe we should wait."

They nodded at each other, almost laughing again with relief. They'd done it. They were here. Now they just needed to wait for the light, and then surely they'd find Pup.

"I reckon we're best off sitting in the canoe, it's too muddy here."

Lissa nodded. The canoe felt like a tiny bit of security, a little piece of home in the middle of the river. "I didn't think about being out in the cold," she admitted. "I should have brought a sleeping bag."

"Me neither," Alfie admitted. "But the cover's in the canoe – we can use that. It's not that wet."

"We can use our buoyancy aids like cushions," Lissa suggested, remembering leaning on hers on top of *Rose Dawn*.

"Hey, I just remembered. I've got something

for you." Alfie stomped back to the canoe and opened up the rucksack he'd tucked in the bow. "Close your eyes a minute."

"It's dark," Lissa pointed out, but she did as she was told, listening to Alfie shuffling about. There was a strange scratch and hissing noise, and then Alfie said, "OK, you can look." He sounded very pleased with himself.

Lissa opened her eyes to see Alfie standing close, his face glowing gold and red in the light of a tiny candle – a birthday candle, stuck in the top of a chocolate muffin.

"I know it's early, but it's still your birthday. Happy birthday, Lissa!"

Lissa was woken by a sharp splash of cold across her cheek and she sat up, shaking herself and spluttering. What was happening? Where was she?

The canoe! They'd fallen asleep in the canoe!

Lissa and Alfie weren't safely beached on the island any longer. There were trails of mist swirling all along the river, but through them Lissa could see open water. They were adrift in the main channel of the river, alone in the grey light of dawn.

"Alfie!" Lissa yelped. "Wake up, Alfie! We're floating!"

Actually, they weren't floating as much as they should be. They'd curled up to wait on the floor of the canoe, heads pillowed on their buoyancy aids, and now there was water in there with them. A lot of it.

Alfie was awake now, staring round in sleep-dazed horror. Then he yelped, "Where are the paddles?"

Lissa looked all over the canoe, lifting the waterproof cover they'd slept on, even peering behind Alfie's rucksack, though she knew it was too small to be hiding the paddles.

"We took them out," she said slowly. "They were getting in the way and we wanted more space. They're back on the island." She turned and looked behind them, but she couldn't see through the mist. She had no idea how far they'd drifted.

"Oh…" Alfie swallowed. "I didn't think the canoe would float away. We pulled it right up the slope, didn't we? I suppose if something big came down the river the wake might have washed us off…" He looked around the canoe again and his face sharpened with panic. "Lissa, we have to bail! There's too much water coming in, we've got to get it out." He searched frantically in his rucksack and handed Lissa a plastic box – the one he'd brought her birthday muffin in. Tears burned at the corners of her eyes, but she scooped water up into the box and flung it over the side, again and again. Alfie did the same with a metal water bottle, but the flood in the bottom of the canoe didn't seem to be going away.

"It's not working," Lissa said desperately, half standing up to reach over the little bench seat. There was a deep bit of water just past it. If she could get rid of that, surely it would help? "Do you think there's a hole? Maybe we put a hole in the canoe when we pulled it up that slope."

"I can't see one," Alfie started to say, then he squawked, "Lissa, be careful!"

But it was too late. Lissa was already teetering as the canoe seemed to shift and sway beneath her feet. Before Alfie could reach out and grab her – before he could do anything – she was in the water.

"Lissa!" Alfie screamed.

Lissa tried to scream too but her mouth was full of water, and it was so cold and shocking that she immediately went under. There was a strange scraping feeling as the cold closed over the back of her neck, then her hair, and everything seemed to disappear. She clutched frantically for the canoe, for air, but it wasn't there. Only water – everywhere – and she couldn't tell which way was up.

Something nudged Lissa's side. For a moment, she thought she'd somehow found the canoe again and she reached out, but then she realized that the something was soft. And it was *pushing* her up.

Lissa broke the surface, gasping and spluttering, and blinked water out of her eyes. She was only a few metres away from the canoe and there was a seal next to her, eyeing her anxiously. A seal with huge, round dark eyes and a head dappled with little leopard spots.

Pup pushed her again, shoving Lissa towards
the canoe with her freckled nose. She couldn't
have said *Get back in that thing* any more
clearly if she'd used words. She shoved Lissa
harder and Lissa nodded.

"I'm going. I promise," she told Pup, too cold and shocked to care that she was talking to a seal. She started to swim slowly and stiffly back towards the canoe, where Alfie was reaching out for her, his face white with panic and his eyes looking even bigger than Pup's.

"Are you all right?" he gabbled as he grabbed Lissa's arm and tried to haul her back in. "I couldn't see you! I didn't know what to do! That's Pup, isn't it? She rescued you!"

"Yeah," Lissa agreed weakly, tumbling into the bottom of the canoe. "She did, didn't she?"

The two of them sat there in the drifting canoe, their eyes fixed on that spotted grey head. The sun was coming up a little brighter now and the dawn light was shining on Pup's smooth fur, glossy with river water. They'd spent so long worrying about her and whether she was all right, thinking they needed to save her – and now Pup had saved Lissa instead.

"Do you think she'd push us over to the bank?" Alfie suggested, and Lissa thought maybe he was only half joking.

"There's something weird about her today," Lissa said. She'd been too frightened and surprised to notice it before, but now she was sure Pup looked different. As though there was something in her mouth, maybe? It looked almost like she had a piece of fish dangling out of it. "Look at her mouth—"

"Lissa!" A shout echoed over the water, and out of the fading mist a boat appeared.

"Dad!" Lissa gasped.

Dad was sitting in the front of a rowing boat, looking more worried than Lissa had ever seen him. Rosy was behind him at the oars – he must have woken her up to borrow the boat.

Rosy drew the boat alongside Lissa and Alfie, and then she spotted Pup in the water. "Look. Someone's come to help them already."

Dad was reaching out to try and hug her, as if he wanted to grab her and haul her back into the rowing boat with him. "Lissa, you're soaked!"

"I fell in," Lissa admitted. "The canoe was half full of water and I fell in while we were trying to bail her out."

"Pup pushed Lissa out of the water," Alfie told Dad and Rosy. "It was amazing. Pup saved her!"

"But what were you doing?" Dad demanded. "Why are you out here in a canoe? Oh…" He looked round at Pup, still watching them solemnly. "You came for her, didn't you? You came for the seal?"

"Let's get them back on dry land," Rosy interrupted gently. "Lissa's soaked through. She needs to get warm and I need a cup of tea."

Dad nodded tiredly. "Yes. Of course. Sorry for dragging you out so early, Rosy… Lissa, pass me that rope. We'll give you a tow."

Rosy pulled them all the way back to *Rose Dawn*. Lissa spent half the time sneaking looks at Dad's set, frightened face, and half of it watching Pup, following after the canoe as if she didn't trust Lissa and Alfie to look after themselves. There was definitely something in her mouth. If it was fish, why didn't she eat it?

The rowing boat bumped up against
Rose Dawn's stern and then Rosy looked
thoughtfully at Dad and Lissa climbing up
on to the bank. "I think I'll have tea back
on my boat, leave you two to talk," she said.
"I'll take Alfie home."

Lissa looked at Dad's serious expression. It
didn't seem like the time to ask Rosy about
Pup's mouth, but she had to.

"Rosy, wait a minute," she burst out. "Look
at Pup. Is there something wrong with her
mouth?"

"Lissa…" Dad said wearily. "Not now."

"It's important, Dad!"

Rosy leaned over the side of her rowing
boat, frowning at Pup, who was watching
them from a couple of metres away.
"Actually, I think Lissa's right. There is

something in the side of her mouth. It looks like a fishing lure to me." She glanced at Lissa. "Anglers use them, to tempt fish to bite. I've got a feeling Pup's got a hook stuck there." She nodded thoughtfully. "Perhaps that's why we haven't seen her... If she was hurt, and wanting to hide herself away..."

"We need to call those divers!" Lissa said anxiously.

Rosy nodded. "Definitely. I'll go and do that now. We can tell them we've just seen the seal and that she needs help."

"Lissa, you need to get out of those wet clothes," Dad said. "Come on."

Lissa swallowed. Dad wasn't going to be happy about this, but they couldn't leave Pup. Not now. "I can't, Dad," she explained, and her voice sounded strangely small but determined. "We've got to stay with Pup. If the rescue team are going to come, they need to know where she is. We can't just let her swim off. Someone has to be watching her all the time."

"Lissa's right." Rosy nodded. "If that is a fishing lure stuck in Pup's mouth, we need to get help for her now. Today."

Lissa watched Dad, watched him close his eyes and then nod reluctantly. She wondered how much sleep he'd had the night before, whether he'd worked till late and then looked in to check on her and found her gone.

"All right. We'll keep watch. You go and call those people, Rosy."

"Yes, as soon as I've dropped Alfie home. I'll let you know what they say. Don't worry, Lissa," Rosy added as she started to row back up the river towards Alfie's houseboat. "She'll be OK. We'll make sure."

Alfie waved at Lissa as they headed off. He waved all the way to the bend in the river, and Lissa waved back.

"We can watch her from the wheelhouse," Dad said, and Lissa followed him back on board the barge. "But Lissa, you need to change first. I promise I'll keep her in sight. And I'll call you if she starts to swim off, OK?"

Lissa glanced uncertainly at Pup, now watching them from just behind the boat. Her dark eyes seemed to be fixed on Lissa and Dad. She didn't look as if she was about to disappear. "All right," she murmured, and she hurried back down to her cabin, throwing on her warmest clothes – showering could wait till later. She probably smelled of river and mud but she didn't care. When she came back up to the wheelhouse, Dad was leaning on the metal frame around the barge's stern, looking down at Pup.

"She hasn't moved," he told Lissa. "It's like she's waiting for you." Then he sighed. "OK then. What happened, Lissa? What made you do it? After all those things I said to you about being careful and sensible. About how dangerous the river can be."

Lissa leaned back against the seat, folding her arms. "You know why I went. You wouldn't help me look for Pup and I was worried about her."

Dad seemed puzzled. "I didn't say I wouldn't help you."

Lissa stared at him, open-mouthed. How could he say that? "Yes, you did! The night before last, that's what we argued about!"

"Oh… Well, maybe. But I was saying not just then, Lissa. I was cooking dinner."

"You said I didn't need to be the one worrying about Pup. You said that, Dad."

Dad sighed again, and his shoulders slumped. "Yes… You're right, I suppose I did. It must have sounded like I wasn't even listening."

Lissa nodded uncertainly. That was *exactly* what it had sounded like. But she wasn't sure how far she could go. How much she wanted to say. If she told Dad what she really felt, she didn't know how he'd react. What if he didn't want her around any more? What if he made her go back to Mum's?

"I missed you!" she burst out at last.

"What? When?"

"All that time after half-term when you

were moving in here and you didn't visit."
Lissa focused hard on Pup's beautiful fan of
whiskers, to stop her eyes filling with tears.
It wasn't working very well. "And then it
was supposed to be special, just us, for the
summer holidays – but it wasn't!"

"Lissa!"

"I know you had to work and it was
important. But it still made me feel like I
didn't matter." She ended on a gasp. There.
She'd told him.

Dad was silent for a moment. "I wanted
everything to be perfect," he muttered at
last. "Your cabin. I wanted you to feel like
you had your own space here, that you
belonged, before you came to see me. I
didn't think – I didn't realize you felt like I'd
abandoned you."

Lissa kept on staring at Pup. "Oh," she whispered.

"And I should have listened more about Pup. I should have known how important she was to you. At least now she's going to get the help she needs, Lissa." Dad took a deep breath. "I should have said no to the work. It wasn't fair."

"You couldn't, though." Lissa shrugged. "You had to do it, for the money."

Dad made a sort of groaning noise. "I could have managed it better. Told the agency I needed to take longer over it, so I could be with you more of the time. Or at least talked to you about things more. I was trying to get it done quickly so we'd have the rest of the holiday together."

Lissa nodded and hesitated for a moment.

She had to tell him – she couldn't just pretend all day. She added in a rush, "And it's my birthday…"

Dad's face was so shocked, she couldn't help her words turning into a wail at the end. He *had* forgotten. And now Lissa really was crying, with great, gulping sobs. She tried to keep watching Pup, even though it was through a haze of tears. They couldn't let her swim away.

Pup didn't seem to want to leave, but she kept opening her mouth as if she was yawning. *She doesn't like the noise of crying*, Lissa thought. She sniffed hard and rubbed her eyes – she had to make herself stop.

"I know it's your birthday, Lissa!" Dad said, staring at her. "Don't cry… Don't look at me like that. I wouldn't forget!"

THE DAWN SEAL

Dad dashed back into the saloon and came out with an armful of presents, all wrapped, with ribbons on. "You can have these now," he said. "Or you might want to wait." He gave her a smug, mysterious, triumphant sort of look.

"Why would I want to wait?" Lissa managed to gasp.

"Ah, well. I can't tell you that. It's a surprise."

Rosy came back along the river path a little
while later and Lissa jumped up, waving at her.
Rosy looked anxiously at the river and smiled
as she spotted Pup.

"She's still with you! That's good."

Lissa nodded. "Did you get through to the
rescue team?"

"Yes, they're coming out as soon as they can,"
Rosy said, sounding relieved. "We're lucky it's a
Saturday. They said they have lots of volunteers
they can call who aren't too far away. And
they said you're doing exactly the right thing

keeping watch over her. Apparently, at lots of their call-outs they spend ages just trying to find the animals they need to help."

"Do you know how long they're going to be?" Lissa asked, glancing anxiously back at Pup. She was further from the barge now, and she'd been moving around more, looking as if she was trying to fish. Lissa hadn't seen her catch anything – she wasn't sure whether she *could* fish, with the lure stuck in her mouth. "The river's going to get busy soon. That's when Pup usually goes..."

"I think she wants to go now," Dad put in. "Look at her. She's moving further away, isn't she?"

"She's going back to the island!" Lissa said. "We've got to follow her!"

Lissa scrambled on to the bank and set

off with Rosy, leaving Dad to lock up *Rose Dawn* and come after them.

They dashed along the path, stopping to peer through the gaps between the boats to check on Pup. She seemed to be heading towards the island, but she darted and dipped and rolled, hardly ever travelling in a straight line.

As they drew
near to the island,
Lissa and Rosy
watched the seal
haul herself out
on to the muddy
patch of beach, and
shuffle behind the
trailing willow branches.
Even though Lissa knew
Pup was there, she could
hardly see her. The seal was
hidden by the willows, her grey-
brown speckled coat camouflaging her
against the mud and pebbles.

"Hopefully she'll stay there for a while,"
Rosy murmured as Dad caught up with them
and Lissa pointed Pup out to him.

Then Rosy's mobile rang, and she scrambled through her pockets to answer it. "Yes? Hello! No, she's moved on, she's hauled out on the little island I mentioned before. Yes, if you come to the Active Water Centre, I'm sure it'll be fine to use their slipway. It's almost opposite the island. Yes, see you soon."

"They're coming?" Lissa said eagerly. "Oh, Dad, please can you text Alfie's mum? I don't want him to miss seeing Pup rescued."

Alfie arrived at a run at almost exactly the same time as a group dressed in a mixture of high-vis, wetsuits and waders, all clearly ready to go in the water.

"I'm the one who called you," Rosy explained. "And this is Lissa and Alfie. They've been watching the seal for the last few days – they're the ones who discovered she was hauling out here, and Lissa noticed she'd got something stuck in her mouth this morning."

Lissa had been wondering if Rosy would say anything about them being out when they shouldn't have been, but somehow she'd managed to be completely truthful and still skate over that bit.

"We think it might be a fishing lure?" Rosy added, and the woman who seemed to be in charge of the group nodded.

"We see quite a lot of those – hooks and lures stuck in seals' mouths. Well done for spotting it, Lissa."

"It's really big," Lissa murmured. "I'm not sure she can catch anything with it there. She disappeared for a couple of days and we wondered if maybe it was because she was scared because she was injured… So she might not have eaten anything for a while," she added worriedly.

"It's great you've managed to keep her in sight, that really helps. I'm Anna, by the way. We'll bring our boats round and see if we can get to her."

"How are you going to catch her?" Lissa asked, biting her lip. She knew that Pup needed help but seeing all these people milling about had made her think how scared the little seal was going to be.

Anna looked thoughtfully at the island. "When we got the message, I was wondering if we could encourage her to head for the lock – we could put a net under the surface of the water and then lift it up around her, you see. But we're actually quite a long way upstream. I'm not sure we can keep her in sight and get her that far."

"We don't think she's keen on the lock either," Rosy agreed. "She hasn't tried to get back through it."

"Mmmm. As she's hauled out on the island, I think we might see if we can catch her here. We've got a crate to put her in." Anna waved at the people carrying inflatable boats and other equipment round from the car park.

Now that the rescue team was here, it felt odd that there was nothing for Lissa, Alfie and Rosy to do to help. Lissa had spent so long worrying about Pup, and now she just had to watch and hope.

"It's weird, isn't it?" Alfie muttered as they watched the three inflatable boats launch. "That's where we were a few hours ago."

Lissa shivered, remembering the canoe and

that terrifying, teetering fall into the water in the dark. And then Pup – that strange little nudge as Pup pushed her up to the surface. It had probably hurt her to do it, with the hook stuck in her mouth. She could still see Pup on the muddy bank, but the seal was shifting nervously, waving a flipper every so often as if she wasn't sure about what was going on.

"Stay there…" Lissa whispered to her across the water. "I know it's scary but please just stay. These people have come to help, I promise. It'll be OK. No one wants to hurt you…"

Some of the rescue team started to climb out into the shallower water where the island sloped to meet the river, carrying what seemed almost like shields.

"What are those?" Dad muttered, peering anxiously at them. Lissa squeezed his hand. He actually sounded worried about Pup too now. She was glad he was there.

"I think they're going to use them to direct her towards that kennel," Rosy said. One of the rescue team was carrying something that looked like a big travel crate for a dog, and he set it down just at the edge of the muddy patch in front of Pup. The little seal was trying to wriggle towards the water, but whichever way she went, one of the rescuers gently moved their board to stop her. It was as though they were making a tunnel towards the crate, and Pup couldn't help but follow it.

Lissa held her breath – *she* was scared, so she couldn't imagine how Pup felt. She almost wanted the seal to escape, to slip past the boards and safely back into the water, but she knew that wasn't right.

"It'll be OK…" she whispered again – and then they heard the metallic snick of the crate's wire door latching shut.

Pup was in.

"Are you in trouble?" Alfie whispered to Lissa, when he found her sitting in the wheelhouse, half asleep in a camping chair after their adventures of the morning and all the excitement of the rescue.

"Not that much. I think Dad's letting me off a bit because it's my birthday, and because he feels like it's partly his fault." She swallowed a huge yawn. "But he hadn't forgotten my birthday! There are presents – he'd hidden them under the benches in the saloon. I think he might be making me a birthday cake too – he said I have to stay out here."

"Is he good at making cakes?" Alfie asked seriously.

"I don't know! He can make pancakes. I've never been with just Dad for my birthday. What about you? What did your mum and dad say?"

Alfie slumped down in the other camping chair and screwed up his face. "I tried getting back in without them noticing but Dad woke up. He was still half asleep and I don't think he understood what was going on until he saw Rosy. She said she'd wait and check whether Mum or Dad wanted to talk to her, you see. I was really worried he was going to be upset about all the water in the canoe and losing the paddles and there maybe being a hole, but he didn't even look at it. He just grabbed me by the shoulders and kept asking me if I was hurt. And I kept saying I was fine, and then Rosy said could she talk to him and told me to go and put the kettle on.

"I don't know what she said, but they were there for ages and when Dad came back in, he made me hot chocolate. Then he said could I not say anything to Mum just yet because she was tired and not feeling great, and he'd tell her when it was the right time." Alfie sighed. "Which is weird because now all I want to do is tell her and I feel really guilty that I can't. But he did make me promise to never, ever take the canoe without him again. He said he'd never even thought of asking me to promise that. And if the canoe's got a hole in it I have to pay for mending it out of my pocket money. And buy new paddles if we can't find them."

"I'll help pay for it!" Lissa said quickly. "I'll have birthday money, my grandad always sends me some."

"Thanks." Alfie grinned at her and then he sniffed thoughtfully. "I can't smell birthday cake."

"No…" Lissa sniffed too. "Me neither."

Just then, the wheelhouse door banged a little, as if a very small fist was hitting it. Lissa and Alfie exchanged a surprised look and went to see what was happening. Lissa was wondering if it was a duck – Dad had told her he'd found a duck in the wheelhouse once, eating half a sandwich that he'd left on the table.

But it wasn't a duck, it was Zoe. Mickey was holding Lissa's little sister up so she could bang on the door.

"Lissa!" she squealed as she saw her sister. "Happy birthday!"

Lissa's mum was behind Mickey, with a box that was almost certainly a birthday cake, and there were bags and bundles stuffed into Zoe's pushchair on the path.

Lissa fumbled with the door catch, laughing. "You came!"

"Your dad called me about a week ago and said he thought you'd like it if we did," her mum explained.

A week ago! Dad *had* been planning after all, while Lissa had been convinced he'd forgotten.

The door next to the wheelhouse opened and Dad came up the steps, looking pleased with himself. "Good surprise?" he said to Lissa.

Lissa hugged him, even though it was tricky with Zoe still hanging on to her leg. "The best. Thank you."

Dad grinned. "You can come into the saloon now. You too, Alfie. I'll text your mum."

Presents, Lissa thought excitedly, helping Zoe down the steps. But she'd seen the presents already, so why had Dad sent her out to the wheelhouse?

She stopped as they came out of the tiny

passage between her cabin and the shower room, gaping at the saloon. It was festooned with flags and fairy lights and enormous paper flowers. The table was piled with presents, and the galley counter was arranged with bowls of crisps and slices of pizza and a huge plate of Lissa's favourite iced ring biscuits.

"Pretty!" Zoe said, turning her head slowly to admire the decorations. "Pretty!"

It *was* pretty. It was the nicest set of decorations Lissa had ever seen. Even her mum seemed impressed and Alfie looked as if he didn't dare touch anything.

"Do you like it?" Dad asked hopefully.

Lissa nodded, smiling at him. She was feeling a strange mixture of happy and guilty all at once. She had been so horrible to Dad while he was thinking about this surprise for her. But then he had broken his promise that they'd spend the holidays together… She wouldn't have been angry if that hadn't happened, would she?

Lissa just didn't know if she was being fair or not. She wasn't sure she ever would. But the hurt, unhappy lump inside her was starting to ease away – Dad wouldn't have done all this if he didn't care about her.

Mum put down the box she was carrying on the bench seat, pulled some more presents out of her bag and added them to the pile on the table. Then she pulled a badge out of her pocket and pinned it on to Lissa's T-shirt. It was huge with a big '10' on it, and it had little flashing lights all around the edge. "Just in case anyone misses that you're ten!" She smiled. "Do you want to open your presents?"

Lissa nodded eagerly. There seemed to be a huge pile now. She opened a rainbow-striped hoodie and a pair of shorts from Mum, Mickey and Zoe. Books and a pencil case full of gel pens from Dad. Rosy had sent her a card with a message that said the binoculars were hers forever, and wishing her many happy days on the river. Alfie had even sneaked in a parcel, a little grey seal that was spotted like Pup. Lissa could see how proud he was that she loved it.

But the best present was an envelope – a big, glittery envelope that looked as though it was home-made. Lissa tore it open curiously and drew out a sheet of paper with a photo of a boat. It looked a bit like a fishing boat. It had *Love from Dad* written on the back, and Lissa frowned at him, puzzled.

"Dad, you haven't bought another boat?"

Dad snorted with laughter. "No! No, I've just hired us a spot on one for the day, later in the summer. She takes people out on seal-watching trips, Lissa. In the Thames Estuary."

"That's where the rescue team are going to take Pup!"

"Yes, it is. I actually booked this a while ago, though – when you were doing all your research into seals. I thought you'd like to go and see more of them." He shook his head.

"Though you've probably had more close-up seal-watching experience over the last couple of weeks than anyone on the boat trips gets, to be honest. They have to be really careful not to get too close and upset them."

"I don't mind." Lissa gripped the photo tightly. "It sounds amazing."

Dad had arranged something so special – so perfect. She might even see Pup, Lissa thought. But there would be hundreds of seals. And maybe she wouldn't recognize Pup among all the others.

I would! Lissa told herself fiercely. *I'd know her anywhere!*

She wanted to believe that Pup would know her too. But in a way, it would be better if she didn't. If Pup forgot all about being so close to people and lived her own wild life, safe in the estuary. Lissa blinked hard. She loved Dad's present, but it was still hard to think about Pup so far away.

"Shall we have your birthday cake?" Mum asked gently, and Lissa gave her a grateful nod. "Why don't you pop outside for a minute? Give me a chance to sort the candles out."

Lissa went up the steps to the wheelhouse and stood looking at the water. It felt empty with no little spotted grey-brown face popping up to look back. Lissa shook her hair briskly, trying to shake away her low mood. It was her birthday! People weren't supposed to be miserable on their birthdays.

She could hear a family walking past on the path, chatting and pointing out the boats to each other. Lissa heard the youngest boy say, in a very obvious whisper, "Look! Look at that girl!

Do you think she *lives* on that boat?"

He sounded so envious that Lissa couldn't help smiling – and she realized that he was right. She did live on a boat. Maybe not all the time, but there would be more summers staying with Dad, wouldn't there? She wanted there to be. More summers waking up at dawn to go out and watch the misty river. Even if she never spotted another seal, she would remember those moments with Pup.

"Lissa! Cake!"

Lissa hurried into the saloon as everyone began to sing. She was dazzled by the ten flickering candles at first, and then she saw that Mum had made her a cake shaped just like Pup. She'd even dappled the icing with little leopard spots.

"I tried to make it so she had her tail up in the air, the way you told me a common seal does, but it was a bit too tricky," her mum explained apologetically.

"It's beautiful!" Lissa told her. "The best cake ever!"

"You'd better blow out the candles," Mum said, looking pleased.

"Don't forget to make a wish!" Alfie said as Lissa sucked in a breath, and she nodded. She knew exactly what she was going to wish for.

She was wishing for Pup. Not to have her back, Lissa knew she couldn't have that, but for Pup to be safe. For the rescue team to take her little dawn seal down the river to the sea, and release her just where she was meant to be.

A little bit of the wish was for Lissa too, Lissa in the future.

For her and Dad, and all the summers on the river to come.

HOLLY WEBB

Holly Webb started out as a children's book editor and wrote her first series for the publisher she worked for. She has been writing ever since, with over one hundred books to her name. Holly lives in Berkshire, with her husband and three children. Holly's pet cats are always nosying around when she is trying to type on her laptop.

For more information
about Holly Webb visit:

www.holly-webb.com